W9-CFJ-441

Alf Saves the Day

ROUND LAKE AREA
LIBRARY
906 HART ROAD
ROUND LAKE, IL 6007
(847) 546-7060

Story by Mal Peet
Pictures by Andy Hammond

dingles & company

Alf loved soccer. He loved everything about soccer.

2

Alf loved drawing soccer pictures. He drew good soccer pictures.

3

Alf loved writing soccer stories. He was good at soccer stories.

Alf loved watching soccer on television.
He cheered and cheered.

Alf loved going to soccer matches.
There were lots of people and
everyone cheered.

Alf was a big soccer fan.

At school, lots of children played soccer.
Lots of boys and lots of girls played.

Alf really, really wanted to be a soccer star. But he wasn't good at soccer.

Some children were good at dribbling.
Alf **wasn't** good at dribbling.

Some children were good at passing.
Alf **wasn't** good at passing.

11

12

Alf was just no good at soccer. He felt very sad.

The soccer coach picked five children for one team. He picked five children for the other team.

Alf went to watch the soccer match.

All the children cheered. The soccer players cheered. The soccer coach cheered.

The lunch lady cheered.

19

The soccer coach said, "Alf, come with me."

Alf stood in the goal and the coach took a shot. It was a good shot, but Alf saved it.

All the children cheered.

Alf was a very good goalkeeper. He **was** good at playing soccer after all!

24